Saxophone Sam and His Snazzy Jazz Band

Christine M. Schneider

Walker & Company ✺ New York

© 2002 Christine M. Schneider

First published in the United States of America in 2002
by Walker Publishing Company, Inc.

Published simultaneously in Canada by
Fitzhenry and Whiteside, Markham, Ontario L3R 4T8

For information about permission to reproduce selections from this book, write to
Permissions, Walker & Company, 435 Hudson Street, New York, New York 10014

Library of Congress Cataloging-in-Publication Data

Schneider, Christine M.
    Saxophone Sam and his snazzy jazz band / Christine M. Schneider.
        p. cm.
    Summary: The sound of toe-tapping dance band music from the radio leads Drew and his
sister throughout their house.
    ISBN 0-8027-8809-2—ISBN 0-8027-8810-6
    [1. Music—Fiction. 2. Dance—Fiction. 3. Big bands—Fiction. 4. Radio—Fiction. 5. Brothers
and sisters—Fiction. 6. Stories in rhyme.] I. Title

PZ8.3.S29718 Sax 2002
[E]—dc21

                                                                                2002016895

Book design by Christine M. Schneider

Visit Walker & Company at www.walkerbooks.com

Printed in Hong Kong

10 9 8 7 6 5 4 3 2 1

For Emmeline

Be bop bop, first a wiggle then a hop!

Time to get things moving, put your tootsies down, start grooving!

Sounds so sweet, do you hear that snazzy beat?

Now's no time to doze—feel the rhythm in your toes!

Yes. You there! Sitting in that bright red chair.

What is that applause? Come investigate the cause!

Rah rah rah! Do you wonder who we are?

Grab your little sister, see if you can find us, mister!

Doo wop wop! Come on, do the lindy hop!

Sam's my name, and, brother, our band's simply like no other.

Through those doors, maybe near the dinosaurs?

Watch us steal the stage as we overtake the page.

Zoom zoom boom! When the day is full of gloom,

Chase away the blues—just put on your dancing shoes!

Where to, boss, since we're not behind the floss?

Maybe there instead, where you rest your weary head.

Zip zed zed, we're not underneath the bed.

Listen, down the hall. Can you tell we have a ball?

Sing, girls, sing! Making music is our thing.

We travel near and far—Yucatán to Zanzibar!

Look, kids, look! Are we hidden in a book?

Wrong again, my friend. Try the stairs around the bend.

Doo dilly dilly, we excel in acting silly!

Follow that cool cat, and you'll find us just like that.

Zoo zoo zing, now the band is in full swing!
Ready for a riddle? Our band's big, but we are little.
Sax, bass, drum, here's our only rule of thumb:
If we're feeling sad, music always makes us glad.

Shoo shoo wink, we're aware that some may think
That we really don't exist, but we do, we must insist!
Zig zug zug. Boy, those kids can cut a rug!
Once they start to wiggle, bet you'll hip-hooray and giggle!

Rat tat tat, we like to dance and that is that.

Polka, shimmy, tango, we can even do fandango!

Me oh my! You can join us, don't be shy.

Dare to take a chance, we just know you'll love to dance!

It's not hard. You don't need a leotard!
Just start to bounce and hop, like the fizz in soda pop.

Zoo zoo wop, let's boogie 'til we drop!

Feel the floorboards shake as the room begins to quake!

KNOCK, KNOCK, KNOCK!

Shhhhh!

Someone's at the door!

Hey! It's Drew, with his little sister, Sue!
Isn't this a treat? You make our audience complete.

Now you know how this broken radio
Still can play hip jazz with incredible pizzazz!

Zip zoo zoo, let's see what you kids can do.
Join us as we jive—music makes us feel alive!

Shoo shoo whee, next we're off to Sicily.

Once that show is through, then perhaps we'll visit you!

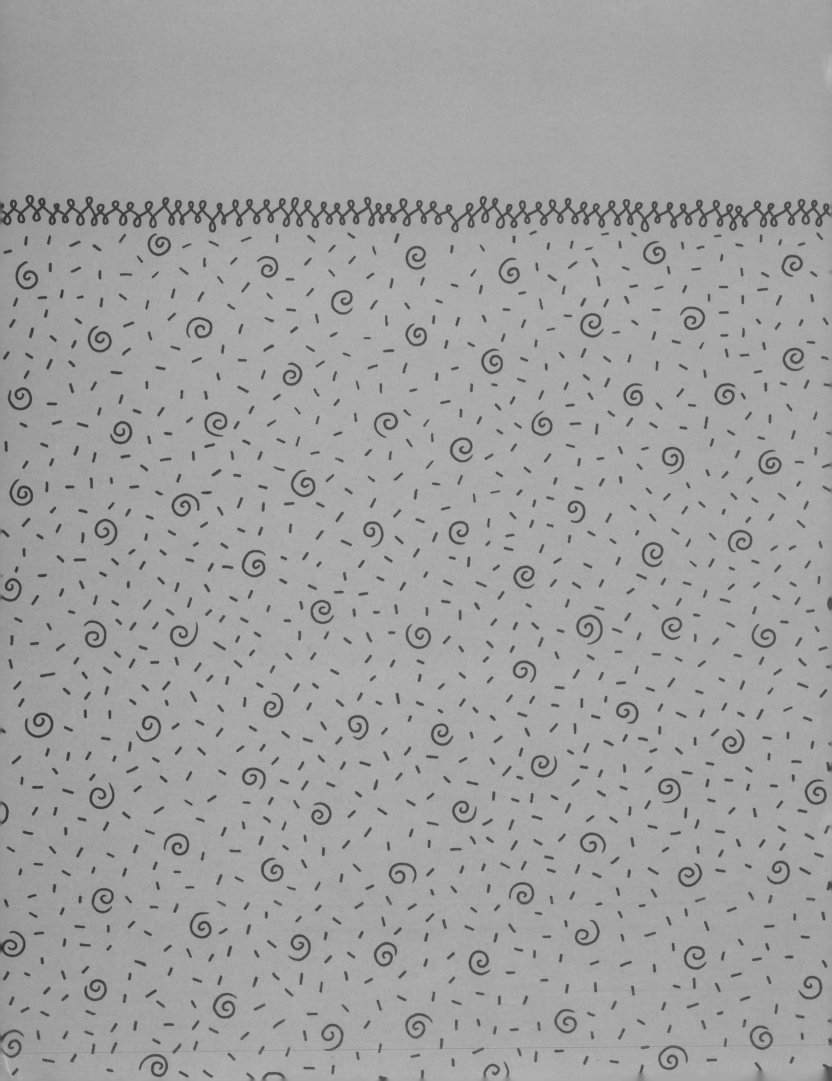